T0367646

BLACK COW

BLACK COW

TAMA

Illustrations by Sarah Brand

authorHOUSE®

AuthorHouse™
1663 Liberty Drive
Bloomington, IN 47403
www.authorhouse.com
Phone: 1-800-839-8640

© 2012 by Tama. All rights reserved.

No part of this book may be reproduced, stored in a retrieval system, or transmitted by any means without the written permission of the author.

Published by AuthorHouse   04/10/2012

ISBN: 978-1-4685-6680-2 (sc)
ISBN: 978-1-4685-6679-6 (e)

Library of Congress Control Number: 2012905035

Any people depicted in stock imagery provided by Thinkstock are models, and such images are being used for illustrative purposes only.
Certain stock imagery © Thinkstock.

This book is printed on acid-free paper.

Because of the dynamic nature of the Internet, any web addresses or links contained in this book may have changed since publication and may no longer be valid. The views expressed in this work are solely those of the author and do not necessarily reflect the views of the publisher, and the publisher hereby disclaims any responsibility for them.

CONTENTS

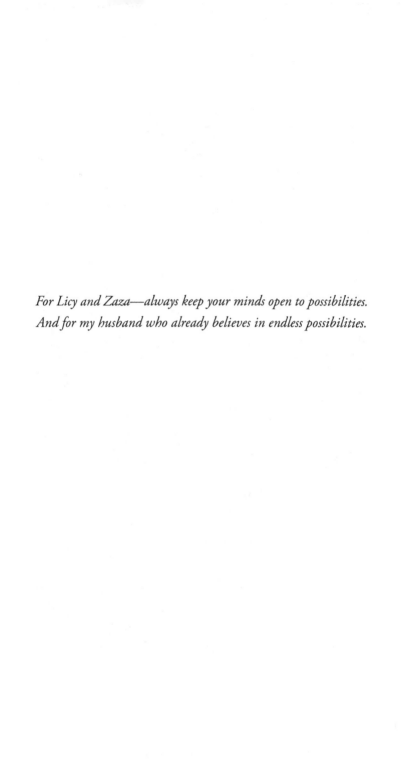

For Licy and Zaza—always keep your minds open to possibilities.
And for my husband who already believes in endless possibilities.

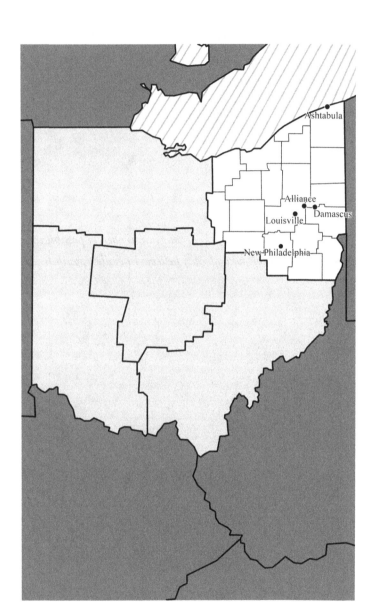

PREFACE

As Alec drove through the winding roads of southern Stark County, his mind wandered to the busy upcoming weeks. He had just finished his last day working for the county park system. It had been a great summer job, but he began to think about his first year of college, which was looming ahead in just three short weeks. Alec had chosen his last day of work to be several weeks before school began so that he could pack up, help his mom around the house and visit with friends before leaving for college in Cincinnati.

The sun had set about a half an hour before and now the night shadows crept out on either side of the road. Dueber Road was a secluded area of Stark County that was surrounded by forest. Alec liked driving this route with the curving roads and scarce traffic.

As he slowed for a curve, he caught a movement out of the corner of his eye. Had someone just moved from beside the huge oak he just passed? Alec slowed down more and peered through his rear view mirror. A branch about eight feet high gently swayed on the huge tree. As Alec quickly reasoned with himself that a bird or squirrel must have just taken off from the branch, he sped back up and his mind returned to the weeks lying before him.

From the woods, a pair of eyes watched as the black Jeep sped away.

CHAPTER 1

Alestair DeWalt was a responsible and independent eighteen year old, looking forward to his first year of college. Alec's parents were divorced, but still got along well. Alec's mom lived in Louisville, a little town famous for being "Constitution town" and where everyone knew everyone. Alec had graduated from Louisville High School just two months before and was looking forward to escaping his small hometown to the vastly larger, and certainly more exciting city of Cincinnati. Alec's dad lived in an even smaller town named Damascus, and that was where Alec was headed tonight. There was a Cleveland Indians game on T.V. and if Alec hurried, he could catch the tail end of it with his dad.

Among other things, summer in Ohio brought lots of road construction, especially on the highways. Because of this, Alec usually took the quiet back roads everywhere that he could. He enjoyed the empty farm roads and appreciated avoiding construction slow-downs and traffic. Alec was surprised and a little annoyed then, when he maneuvered down Parks Road to see police cars blocking the road. He knew it wasn't construction because he drove this way regularly. Had to be an accident.

Jeez, by the time he got turned around and went down another road, he'll loose a good ten minutes in getting to his dad's house.

Alec pulled his old black Jeep to a stop and decided to make sure the accident didn't involve anyone that he knew before he turned around. He was just outside Louisville and his mom would want to know details about any accident that shut down a road. As he hopped out of his car, a state trooper came toward him from the car blockade on the road.

"Hey officer," Alec said lightly. He didn't want to seem nosey. "I, uh, work for the parks . . . is there anything I can do to help? Is everyone OK?" As Alec spoke, he glanced past the flashing lights and saw a red pick-up on the road. It looked like the front passenger's side had smashed into something. Weird, Alec thought as he looked around. Both sides of the road were covered in cornfields—no trees anywhere nearby. And there didn't seem to be a second banged up car.

"Everything's fine, son" the trooper replied. "You can turn around. This road will be closed for another thirty minutes or so."

"Ok" said Alec, still peering around the lights to see the crushed side of the pickup. "Hey, what happened? Corn stalks couldn't have made that dent."

The trooper pulled at his hat. "A black cow was crossing. You need to go now, son. We don't want traffic building up. There's enough room to back up and turn around right behind you."

Alec sensed that he wasn't going to get any more information and the trooper seemed to want him gone. Mom would just have to read about the details in the paper, if this was even important enough to make the police report.

As Alec headed back the way he came, he wondered where the cow was. It couldn't have survived that crash, at least not without being really injured. And whose cow was wondering through cornfields and into roads?

CHAPTER 2

By the time Alec got to his dad's house, his mind had already wondered back to the weeks ahead and he forgot to mention the cow accident to his dad. As he entered the small house off Seacrist Road, Chet DeWalt looked up from the stack of papers in front of him. The Indians game was still on T.V., but Alec's dad seemed more focused on the pile that was scattered on the coffee table in front of him.

"What's all this?" Alec inquired as he dropped into the recliner.

"Oh," replied Chet "I'm just getting around to looking through some of your grandfather's stuff." Alec's grandfather, like Alec's dad, had worked as a zoning officer. When Alec was little, Grandpa Henry had died in a car accident while taking some paperwork to Cleveland. Alec's dad, Chet, had been devastated. This was back when Alec's mom and dad were still married, and Alec vaguely remembered how unhappy everyone seemed to be during that time. Chet had lost his only remaining parent and was in an unhappy marriage. Alec's mom, Gina, had been just as unhappy. After Grandpa Henry's belongings were sold off and given away, Chet and his sister Char had been left with several boxes of personal items. Char traveled a lot then, so Chet got left with storing the boxes. At the time, his life was pretty complicated. So the boxes got put in the attic of Chet's new home when he moved out. Alec remembered that year well because he had been thrown into a world of joint custody and two homes.

Chet himself had retired two weeks ago from his position as Stark County zoning director. He was still slowly moving out of his office at the county building while helping the new director get settled into the job. But, he clearly now had enough spare time to begin filtering through his house and working on projects that had been put aside for years.

"Cool . . . anything interesting?" asked Alec.

Chet smiled and held out a stack of photos for Alec to look through. For the next hour, Alec and his dad looked through photos, laughed and recalled some funny stories about Grandpa Henry. They hardly noticed that the Indians lost the game.

Finally, Alec felt his eyes getting the familiar grainy feeling of sleepiness. He had a long last day of work at the park, and it had caught up with him.

"I think I'm done for tonight Dad." Alec yawned.

"Ok" replied Chet "I'm going to go through a few more things here. See you in the morning."

Alec went to his room, lied down, and forgot about all the events of his day as he dozed off.

CHAPTER 3

When Alec woke up the next morning, Chet was already up brewing coffee. As Alec yawned and stretched his way into the kitchen, Chet asked with a smile, "So, what are you going to do with your first day of unemployment?"

"Don't know." Alec replied while rubbing his eyes. "Do you want to go fishing or something?"

Chet furrowed his brows in thought. "I'd love to, but I came across some papers that I need to take over to the office."

"Ok, no big deal." replied Alec. "I'll figure out something to do. I have naps to catch up on, if nothing else."

Chet grinned. "I'm sure you'll come up with something more productive than that." He gathered up a stack of papers and patted Alec's back. "See you later—lock up if you leave."

After Chet left, Alec wandered into the living room with a cup of coffee. He really didn't enjoy the taste of the coffee, but it helped him wake up and made him feel grown up. So, he kept trying to get used to it.

Alec sat on the couch. Chet had left his wristwatch on the table next to the stack of Grandpa Henry's papers.

7

As Alec looked at the stack, he thought "Dad was looking through papers from grandpa . . . what zoning work did he think of that suddenly needed taken care of?" Chet had seemed really interested in going through the boxes that were strewn across the living room. It seemed odd that he would think of something that needed his urgent attention when he was now newly retired. Whatever, thought Alec. He had too many other things to think of besides trying to figure out what was going on in his dad's head.

After abandoning his coffee, Alec decided to start his first day off with a breakfast at his favorite morning spot, The Sunrise Diner on Route 173. He went to the counter and ordered his usual—pancakes and sausage with O.J. He ate by himself and enjoyed knowing that he had no plans for the rest of the day. As he finished, he noticed a dark haired girl at the other end of the counter. She was very pretty and she was looking at him. Alec's first thought was that he had a piece of food stuck to his face or his hair was messed up. But as he casually wiped at his face, he noticed that she was looking at him intensely, and with a smile. Wow, thought Alec, this may be the start of a really good day.

Although Alec was good looking in his boy-next-door way, he was a quiet person and didn't often have beautiful girls eyeing him. Alec timidly smiled back. The girl apparently took Alec's smile as an invitation. She walked over and seated herself beside him.

"Hi, I'm Lila." the girl introduced herself. "I was hoping to talk to you, if you have a few minutes."

"Um, ok." Alec replied. Maybe she was one of those people who stopped other people for surveys or something.

"Great! I'll meet you outside." Lila hopped off the counter stool and swayed out the door.

Alec's curiosity was poking at every nerve as he quickly paid his bill and walked outside. He spotted the girl and began walking over. As he got near, Alec gasped. Lila was standing next to a pick-up. A red pick-up with a smashed in front side.

"Wow," said Alec "I'm surprised that this can be driven with the way the side is banged up."

"Yeah," replied Lila "the sheriff's office kept it overnight. I need to take it to the shop to get fixed now. But I wanted to show you first and ask what you saw."

Alec was confused. "First, how did you know I was here? And how did you know I was there last night?"

Lila looked uncomfortable. "I just knew. Let's just leave it at that right now. But, you were the only car to come down that road while my truck and I were there last night. What did you see?"

Alec thought about the encounter with the officer on the road surrounded by cornfields. "I don't know . . . a smashed up pick-up, sheriff's cars . . . I didn't even see you."

Lila pressed for more. "Did you see my truck? Did you see anything on it?"

Alec shook his head. This girl was creeping him out a little. "I wasn't that close and it was getting dark. Why?"

Lila looked hesitantly at her truck and back to Alec. "Look, I know that we don't know each other—but I think that you're the one I need to talk to about this." She moved closer to Alec and looked up at him with her startlingly green eyes. "I was driving down Parks Road and this big hairy thing came out from the corn stalks. I saw its face before my truck hit it. I slammed the brakes, but couldn't stop quick enough on the gravel road . . . and it hit my front side. I heard a terrible howl—like a person in pain. I jumped out of my truck, obviously without thinking of any possible danger, and ran around the side in time to see cornstalks move as it ran back in. I got back in my truck and called 911 . . . I wasn't sure at that point if I had hit a bear or a person or what. I stayed in my truck until the sheriff's cars got there. When I saw the flashing lights, I got out and walked around to the passenger side so that I could describe what happened. It was then that I saw the blood on my truck . . . along with what looked like a patch of long black hair caught in the fender. It was too long for bear fur—and there aren't even too many bears in Ohio. The first officer there took me to his cruiser and made me tell what happened in detail, and then he kept asking questions. I started thinking that I had hit a person . . . this thing was tall . . . it could have been a very tall person. Anyway, the one officer drove me home and told my father that he drove me because I had bumped my head—which I didn't. Then told my dad that I could pick up my truck this morning. When we got to the sheriff's department, my truck was totally clean. No blood, no hair—they washed the whole thing. Now, I know that police do a good job . . . but since when do they detail the exterior of trucks in minor traffic accidents? And if I bumped my head, why didn't they take me to the hospital?" Lila's eyes were wide as she took a deep breath and looked around the parking lot before continuing. "Anyway, I asked them this morning what I had hit. They told me it was a black cow . . . a stray black cow. What the heck? The hair on my fender was too long for a cow . . . gosh, I've lived in farm country my whole life! I know cows and I know what are not cows. Even if it vaguely resembled a cow—it would have been one humongous heifer to be what I saw. And, I think I saw whatever I hit get up on two legs. Not cow behavior. Maybe a bear could do that. There was that black bear that was hit in Marlboro Township awhile back . . . but the hair didn't match and even a bear would not have been that big. They gave me paperwork for my insurance company stating that I had a collision with a cow—but it doesn't make any sense. They blocked off the road, drove me home instead of calling my parents, then kept and *cleaned* my truck . . ." Lila trailed off after her rambling. "So I was hoping that you saw something to help me feel like I'm not crazy."

Alec took a deep breath as he took in all that Lila had said. "Maybe you *did* hit your head?" Lila glared at him.

"Ok," started Alec "that's a lot of information. Um, I did wonder about the black cow bit when the officer told me that last night."

"What?" asked Lila "They told me that they confirmed it was a cow later on. But they told you right there at the accident that it was a cow?"

"Yeah" said Alec. "Weird. But just as weird is how you knew me and where to find me this morning. Can we talk about that now?"

Lila ignored the question. "Can you come with me? I need to drop off this truck and go tell all of this to my brother." Her sparkling green eyes peered at Alec as she brushed back her dark hair.

Alec thought that this girl was a little nutty and this whole story is odd . . . but heck, he had no other plans. Besides, hanging out with a pretty girl isn't the worst way to spend a free day.

"Sure" Alec replied. "Where exactly does your brother live?"

CHAPTER 4

Alec and Lila dropped the red pick-up off and headed toward Lexington Township, where Lila's brother lived. Her brother Sam was nineteen and just bought his own place. On the way, Alec's cell phone rang—it was Chet just leaving the zoning office.

"Alec, I have to make some stops and may not make it back until late. Go stay with your mom tonight, ok?" Chet said through the phone.

"Alright," replied Alec "but you know I don't mind being alone."

Chet quickly responded "No, no—go stay with your mom. I'll call you by tomorrow morning. I need to send a package off to your Aunt Char and then stop at the bank before heading north."

Alec cut him off "Dad, where do you have to go? Your retired, remember?"

Chet gave a chuckle "Yeah, I remember. Boring stuff about where and why I'm traveling . . . I'll explain later if you're still interested."

"Ok" Alec replied "I'll definitely talk to you by tomorrow."

As Alec hung up, Lila directed him to the small brick house on Eberly Drive. A tall, dark haired guy was mowing the lawn, but turned the mower off as he saw the car pull in. Lila hopped out of the Jeep and skipped over to hug the man who was obviously her brother. He had the same green eyes and dark hair that Lila had, but the shape of his face was slightly different.

Sam had a subtle look of having a Native American heritage. His cautious eyes and darkened skin matched that of the older man sitting on his porch. As Alec exited the Jeep, he wasn't sure what was expected of him at this point. Did Lila want him to just drop her off?

"Alec," sang Lila "Come meet Sam." Lila made her introductions, then Sam looked over to her and asked "What's going on? Something happened?" Sam seemed very attuned to Lila. Lila gave him a small smile and lead them both to the porch where she introduced Alec to their Uncle Brooks. Lila explained that Uncle Brooks was known as "Chief Manitou" and he gave talks around the area about America Indian culture and native history. Alec made a mental note that he had been right about the Native American features he saw in Sam.

After the small talk, Lila recounted the events of last night to her brother and uncle. She continued the story by adding that she went to see Alec this morning to find out what he saw and because she said he was "part of all this." Alec was still perplexed and wondered what the heck she meant. But before he could ask anything, Sam chuckled at the look Alec apparently had on his face.

"Dude, like it or not, you are now involved in whatever is going on with my sister," Sam turned to Lila "You should let him in on your freak-ability, Lila."

Lila rolled her green eyes. "Okay . . . Alec, you wanted to know how I found you this morning and how I know you, right? Well, I know it sounds psycho, but I just *know* stuff. I felt your presence at the accident last night—certain people have an energy that I can feel really well. Then this morning, I just kind of knew where you would be." Lila shrugged "Please don't think I'm creepy—I just can feel energy from people sometimes."

"And see energy too," Sam added as he looked at Alec "she reads auras—sees the energy that people put out. You know, negative, positive, fearful . . . she doesn't notice it much anymore because it's second nature. She just avoids the negative auras and really only notices if someone has a really distinct aura or energy."

"It's not a big deal." Lila brushed off the explanation.

Alec was a little weirded out with this whole day. But a thought came to him even as he was trying to wrap his mind around exactly what Sam had said.

"Lila, did the animal you hit last night have an aura?"

Lila looked surprised. "I . . . I . . . let me think. I don't usually get strong auras off animals. But I did feel and see fear in the brief instant that it was in my view. I guess with my adrenaline and all, I assumed that the fear was mine, but it could have very well been from . . . whatever it was that I hit."

"You could confuse your own aura with someone else?" Alec was curious now.

"Just, like, in really intense situations and when something happens fast. Like memories . . . the feelings and auras get a little tangled in my brain."

Sam looked over at Uncle Brooks. "This little adventure sounds like something 'Chief Manitou' would tell a story about." Sam smirked "Do *you* know what Lila could have hit and why the police acted the way they did?"

Uncle Brooks smiled gently. "You kids have heard me talk about spirit watchers—maybe Lila saw one. I'm sure you'll figure it out. I have a visitor stopping by this afternoon, so I have to be on my way."

Sam looked at Alec "Uncle Brooks lives in Ashtabula, so he's got a little drive to get home."

"Is it 'Chief Manitou' business?" asked Sam with a half smile.

Uncle Brooks looked pointedly at Sam. "I believe that it is. Alec, it was nice to finally meet you." And with that Uncle Brooks waved good-bye as he got in his old car and backed out.

But Alec's head started spinning again. Why did Lila's uncle say it was nice to *finally* meet him?

CHAPTER 5

After Uncle Brooks left, Alec decided to try to get a few questions of his own answered.

"So Lila, why aren't you telling all of this to your parents? Why didn't I drive you home? You're only, like, sixteen right? Maybe you should be home." Alec pressed.

"I'm seventeen and my parents don't care if I'm here with Sam. They both work long hours and wouldn't listen to me anyway." Lila replied.

Sam interjected, "For sure, they are good people, but they are very . . . practical, grounded . . . close-minded. They both turned their backs on our Native American heritage a long time ago. We can visit with Uncle Brooks, but neither mom or dad speak to him. They think he's flaky and 'making a mockery of our family's background'—so Lila is best to keep them out of her little drama . . . unless something specifically criminal has gone on."

"Ok, and why did Brooks say that it was nice to *finally* meet me? What was that about?" Alec asked.

Sam and Lila looked at each other and both shrugged. "I have no idea, man." Sam said honestly. "Uncle Brooks is just different sometimes. I wouldn't think much of it."

Alec chatted with Lila and Sam for a while longer before making his excuses to leave. He had a lot of information thrown at him today and he needed to go home and sort it all out. Lila walked Alec to his car.

"Hey, thanks for everything today—I know I come off as a little odd . . ." she faltered.

"No, no," said Alec as he looked at her blushing face. "This has been an interesting day . . . weird, but interesting." he smiled.

"Well, anyway," she blushed deeper, "I'll make it up to you—maybe a picnic? Once I get my truck back that is."

Now it was Alec's turn to blush, "That sounds great." he replied with a lopsided grin. Odd or not, Lila was beautiful and interesting. Alec was intrigued with her. Even though she apparently knew how to find him, they exchanged cell phone numbers and said their goodbyes.

☆   ☆   ☆

As Alec made the drive from Lexington Township back to Louisville, his head was swimming. About half way to his mom's house, he noticed that his phone light was blinking—a text message waiting. He had left his phone in the car while at Sam's house, so the message could have come anytime while he was there.

He clicked on to his message screen and read, *"Al—the mounds are the key. check Henry's work papers for"*

It cut off—that was it. It was from his dad. Alec tried to call Chet, but got no answer. He decided to go to his dad's house—he wouldn't stay, but he wanted to figure out what he was suppose to check for.

☆   ☆   ☆

Alec parked in front of his dad's house and jogged up to the front door. As he put his key in the lock, the door pushed open. Alec was very sure he had locked it when he left earlier.

"Hello?" he called. Alec heard what sounded like a click of the back door. Chet had said to go to mom's house . . . but what about the text? From the doorway, Alec eyed the pile of Grandpa Henry's papers. He also noticed his dad's watch face down on the carpet. It had been carefully set on the coffee table this morning when Alec had coffee. Alec didn't think his dad had been back home and he knew that *he* didn't knock the watch to the floor. He brushed past the piles of photos and grabbed the big box stuffed with work papers. Alec made sure that the door was locked and then hurried to the car. Then, he cautiously went to the back door and tried it—it was locked. The click he heard was either in his imagination, or someone locked the door when they left. Alec was getting too creeped out to stay and find out.

As he went back to his car, Alec tried his dad's cell phone again. No answer. Should he call the police? No, he didn't even know what was going on—what the heck would he tell the police? He didn't want to look like a big doofus.

Alec quickly loaded up the box of papers and headed to his mom's house. As he left, he called his dad's cell phone again and left a message. *"Call me as soon as you can—I think someone was in your house."*

CHAPTER 6

Gina DeWalt was watering the flowers on the porch of her white split-level when Alec pulled up and hopped out of his Jeep.

"Hey sweetie!" she smiled. "I wasn't expecting you—what a nice surprise!"

Alec gave his mom a peck on the cheek. The good part about having two homes was that parents were usually happy to see him since he wasn't in one place all of the time.

"You look a little worried," Gina frowned "what's up?"

Alec decided that he didn't want to concern Gina with the weirdness of the past day. "I'm just getting use to not having a job anymore . . . and no school for a few weeks. I'm not sure what to do with my time!" he joked.

Gina smiled "Oh, I can help with that. Just go look at that room of yours. Cleaning that mess will take some time." Gina was a great mom and she babied Alec in many ways. But she drew the line years ago at cleaning his room for him. Alec had been so busy all summer that he knew the room was a huge mess. "I'm on it right now," Alec smiled. Might as well do something productive while his brain was swirling with the events of the day.

Before starting the task of cleaning up his room, Alec hauled up the papers that he had taken from his dad's house. Fortunately, Gina was busy chatting with the neighbor and she didn't notice what he took out of his Jeep.

Alec dropped the box of papers on top of the pile of clothes covering his bed and he sighed. Clean and make mom happy, or read and figure out what's going on? The dirty clothes weren't going anywhere and Alec couldn't resist his curiosity. He shuffled through the paperwork . . . some certificates for training his grandfather had done, cards, random invoices . . . basically nothing interesting. He found a zoning report book with some pages ripped out, but that didn't tell him anything. So Alec went on.

There were a few pictures and personal letters in the stack, but Alec was getting discouraged. He picked up an old birthday card and smiled at the goofy picture on the front when he felt something sticky on the back. He flipped the card over—Grandpa Henry must have set this on icing or something. There was a scrap of ripped paper stuck to part of the sticky area that Alec absentmindedly removed and turned over. On the back were two lines of script that read:

Ironton Register 551892
Adams County mounds

The rest of the paper was ripped off, but the second line caught Alec's attention—mounds.

This was the closest thing to a clue that he had gotten. Alec put the scrap aside and continued to search through the rest of the paperwork with no luck at finding anything more helpful. He went back to the scrap . . .

Ironton Register 551892
Adams County mounds

He went to the computer that Gina had gotten for him four years ago for his room. Alec logged on and typed Adams County mounds in the search engine. The first choice was *Adams County, Washington*. Nope—that's not it. The second was *Great Serpent Mound in Adams County, Ohio*. Bingo. Alec clicked on to the site. It told about the serpent mound in southern Ohio. Apparently effigy mounds were from the Adena people. There was speculation about what they may represent. But Alec still couldn't see what this had to do with his dad . . . or his grandfather. Mounds and ancient people. What is the connection between that and why he can't reach his dad . . . or between that and his grandfather's old paperwork? In the back of Alec's mind, he knew there was something—but he couldn't grasp what the connection could be. Maybe the first line of the note would be helpful.

He typed in *Ironton Register*. The Ironton Tribune webpage came up with a notation that the "Register" was it's previous name. It was a small town newspaper. What was 551892? Maybe an issue number or part of a phone number for the paper? Like many small business websites, there was not a lot of information provided. Alec put his mind to problem solving . . . and it came to him. His job with the parks could lead him to the right place to figure out what he needed to know!

CHAPTER 7

To make Gina happy, Alec quickly cleaned up his room—putting pretty much everything either under his bed or in the laundry. While he was working, he dialed the county library. The parks had offices in the Sippo Center—which shared space with a branch of the county library. When Alec had time during the summer, he would pop into the library to check out movies. Since college was going to take a lot of his money, he was saving as much as he could, and the library lent movies for free. From the frequent stops in, Alec had gotten to know a few of the librarians well.

"Stark County Library," a pleasant voice answered. Alec knew the voice right away.

"JoAnn? This is Alec from the parks . . ."

"Oh, hi Alec!" JoAnn replied "what movie are you looking for today? I can hold something for you . . ."

Alec interrupted "Thanks JoAnn, but I'm actually looking for some information on a newspaper today."

"That's a new one for you, but you know I'll be glad to help." JoAnn said.

"It's the Ironton Register . . . or Tribune." Alec told her.

"Let me look." she said, and Alec heard tapping computer keys in the background. "Yep, we have this on microfiche—you'll have to come in to use the machine if you want to see this paper."

"Great!" said Alec "Give me twenty minutes . . ."

"Uh, Alec," JoAnn interjected "we close in 10 minutes." Alec looked at the clock—ten 'til eight. Where had the day gone?

"Oh, sorry" Alec replied. "Ok—I'll be in first thing in the morning."

JoAnn asked, "Is there a certain article, issue number, date, year . . . ? So I can get out what you need."

Alec thought a minute. "Would there be an issue number 551892?" Alec heard JoAnn clicking away on her computer.

"No . . . these aren't catalogued by issue numbers, just by date and by our catalogue numbers."

"Do you have a catalogue number . . ." Alec started when she cut him off.

"No hon, our microfiche numbers use a letter and number catalogue system." Joann answered.

Alec had a thought for a moment. "How about I R 551892?"

"Nope. 3 letters and 3 numbers are in the system." JoAnn added "Could your number be a date?"

Alec looked at the number, "I don't see how."

JoAnn sounded a little impatient now, "5 . . . the month of May, 5 . . . 5th day . . . 1892 for the year"."

Alec was surprised, "Is the newspaper that old?"

"Yep" She continued, "it looks like this paper started in 1850."

"Ok then," Alec replied with a new sense of excitement, "lets look at that date—first thing tomorrow."

CHAPTER 8

Alec knew that the library opened at nine AM, so at eight-thirty he was bounding down the steps.
"Bye mom. Be back later." Alec called.

"Whoa!" Gina yelled "I've barely seen you—what are you doing today?" She was trying to be friendly and interested in his life, but Alec was in a hurry. So he gave a quick answer. "Just some stuff to get ready for school. I'll be back around in a little bit." He grabbed a banana and dashed out the door before she could ask anything else.

Alec got to the library and waited until exactly nine o'clock. As he walked in the door, JoAnn greeted him with a smile.

"Hey! You *are* here first thing!" She led Alec to the old audio visual room. "I have the film for that date out for you." She showed Alec how to use the microfiche machine, then left to go back to the front desk. Alec began searching. The newspaper had lots of advertisements . . . apparently marketing has always been a big part of the media, thought Alec. He scanned marriages, deaths and a local farm report. He started to fidget, getting impatient with the lack of interesting information. Keep going, he thought . . . there must be something interesting. He began tediously reading an article on local history titled "Indian Legends Meet Present Day Construction."

> *Where Proctorville now stands was at one time a part of a well-paved city, but the greatest part now is the Ohio River. Only a few mounds there; one of which was near the Wilgus mansion and contained the skeleton of a very large person, all double teeth in a jaw bone that would go over the jaw with flesh on, of a large man. The common burying ground was well filled with skeletons at a depth of about six feet.*

Mounds. Large person. Burying ground. Too many thoughts were swirling in Alec's head. He read more . . .

> *. . . Evidence for the occupation of this region before the appearance of the red man and the white race is to be found in almost every part of the county, as well as through the northwest generally. In removing the gravel bluffs for the construction and repair of roads, and in excavating cellars, hundreds of human skeletons, some of them of giant form, have been found.* ***

Mounds. Construction and excavating . . . jobs that the zoning department would be involved with. Chet . . . dad . . . how was he connected? Another realization was gnawing at Alec's mind. Red men. Large human skeletons. Lila was part Native American and she had hit something large . . .

The ring of his phone jolted Alec back to the present. He looked at the caller—Lila. Maybe she *did* pick up on energy—had she known that he was thinking of her?

***alleged Ironton Register quotes were taken from Giants of Ohio (see references)

CHAPTER 9

"Lila?" Alec answered "What's up?"

"I thought I'd visit with you since you are at the library. Only, I don't see you." she answered.

"You're at the library?" Alec questioned.

"Yeah and so are you . . . but where?" Lila replied.

Alec was getting officially freaked out. "Is this one of those things that you *just know* . . . that you found me at the library? Because I've got to tell you, it is getting a little creepy."

Lila laughed "Actually I was just returning some books and I saw your Jeep in the lot. But if you want to think I'm stalking you . . ."

"No, I feel better about coincidence than mind reading, or whatever it is you do. I'm finishing up in the audio-visual room now—I'll meet you at the front desk." finished Alec.

Alec printed off the pages of the article from the microfiche machine, folded them up and set off for the front desk. Lila was chatting with JoAnn. Apparently this was something else they had in common—a friendship with the local librarian. As Alec approached, JoAnn looked up and smiled, "Did you find what you need Alec? Or can I get you a different film?"

"I found some good information" Alec replied guardedly. "But, do you have any books specifically about local Indian legends . . . and maybe how legends may have something to do with, um, construction?"

JoAnn looked dubious. "Indian legends, yes. Indian legends with construction? I can't think of any, but let me look for you." JoAnn walked away and Lila looked at Alec curiously. "Have I inspired you enough with my Native American background that you want to look up legends now?" She asked with a curious smile.

"Actually, you may have something to do with what I'm looking for. But mostly, I'm researching some information I found with my dad's things. In the process, I had an idea about what you may have hit out on Parks Road the other night."

Before Lila could ask more, JoAnn came back with a handful of books on Ohio Indians and folklore. "These should at least get you started on whatever it is you're looking for. What *are* you looking for Alec?" JoAnn inquired.

Good question, thought Alec. Am I trying to figure out where my dad went, am I trying to figure out what Lila hit or is there more?

Alec just smiled, "I'm still figuring out what information I need. If I have any specific topic, you know that you are my first call."

"Well sweetie, you let me know what else I can do to help." A little girl was ready to check out some books, so JoAnn started to turn away. "You kids have a good day . . . and tell your uncle I said hello, Lila."

"Sure thing!" Lila replied, as she and Alec walked out.

As they walked out into the August sunshine, Lila tentatively said "You know, if you need to know about Indian legend, my Uncle Brooks specializes in that, remember?"

Alec *had* thought of it, but felt his ideas were too wild and disconnected to put on someone else's lap just yet. Before he could reply though, Lila added "Even things that seem like a puzzle can be clearer with another set of eyes. When I was really little and only knew my numbers up to 5, I remember doing a dot-to-dot picture where I drew lines from 1 to 2, 2 to 3, 3 to 4 and 4 to 5. I didn't know for sure what 6 looked like, so Sam finished the puzzle up to 10. Together, we made the outline picture of a boat. But, without him, the picture would not have looked like anything."

"Why did you just tell me that?"

Lila shrugged and smiled "Just a hunch."

Alec nodded his head and smiled back. Maybe he could use some help here. "Ok. Let's go see if Sam or Uncle Brooks can help with my puzzle."

CHAPTER 10

Lila followed Alec back to his house, and then he got in her rental car with her so that they could ride together. Along the way, Alec learned that Lila's Native American background made her part Wyandot. And he learned a little more about how her parents did not talk about their heritage so Uncle Brooks, her mom's brother, was the only person that she and Sam could learn from.

At Sam's house, Alec sat down and explained all the pieces of his discombobulated puzzle. His dad was missing after looking through old zoning papers. His grandfather had died while on a zoning job and that is where the papers came from. Someone had been in his dad's house . . . he was sure of that now. He found the scrap of paper. Then he told them about his trip to the library and pulled out the paper he had copied from the microfiche article. Sam and Lila each read it, both connecting dots in their own heads. Alec finished by saying, "And then I had to wonder if I found a connection to what Lila hit with her pick-up."

"Wow," said Sam. "I'm not totally sure what direction to go with this."

Lila added, "I see dots, but I'm not sure how to connect them just yet." She smiled her brilliant smile at Alec.

Sam was on board to figure this out. If for no other reason, he would help because his sister was involved and a man was missing. Sam couldn't turn his back on that. "I'll go see Brooks. There is an awesome library at the Native American Center and I can do some Internet research too."

"Great," said Alec "the only other place I can think to look at is my dad's office."

"I thought he retired?" questioned Lila.

"He did. But he's helping his replacement get use to the job and he is slowly moving out of his office in the process. It took my dad years to go through my grandfathers belongings, the man does not do things quickly."

Lila straightened up "Well then, let's go help him."

☆   ☆   ☆

With Sam on his way to Ashtabula to see Brooks, Lila and Alec headed to the zoning office. When they entered, the receptionist, Sue, greeted Alec kindly. "Well, there's the college boy!" she smiled. "Are you ready to go?"

"Not quite yet, but I guess I'll need to be ready soon" Alec smiled at the woman. "I need to get in my dad's office, if that is alright."

Sue looked at Alec, then at Lila and back to Alec. "Well, he's not here . . . he must be enjoying his retirement too much to finish cleaning out that office" she gave a little laugh. "Why do you need to go in it?"

Alec thought quickly. "He mentioned missing his gold watch. I was in the area and told him I'd stop and see if he left it in his old office. And maybe I can organize a few of his things to help get him out of there sooner." He winked at Sue. Alec knew that Sue liked things to get done. Any help clearing out an office would make Sue happy. And

Alec had a good reason for the stop, even though he knew perfectly well that his dad's watch was at home on the floor, where Chet would never have left it.

Sue gave a conspiratorial smile. "Ok. I guess he could use a little help with all his stuff. You're a nice boy to help your dad out Alec."

"Thanks," Alec smiled again at her. If she only knew that he was really trying to find where his dad was. Does a good son leave his dad missing?

Lila and Alec began scouring the office. They found oodles of boring zoning paperwork, some fairly current take-out menus and lots of things they would both categorize as *junk*. But nothing that would help connect their dots. After being in Chet's office long enough to probably make Sue curious, they decided they better leave. To cover his story, Alec threw some papers in a box and carried them out, waving a "thanks" to Sue on the way.

Having nowhere else to go they drove along and discussed the information they already knew. Although the drive seemed aimless, neither were surprised when they found themselves on Parks Road.

Lila parked at the same place where her pick-up sat the other night. "Back to the scene of the crime" she joked.

The pair got out and began walking to the cornfield. There were stalks stomped down and bent over, but deer or people could have done it. No evidence of anything weird.

"You know how I just *know* things?" asked Lila, without waiting for an answer she continued. "Well, there is something about all of this that I know . . . but it's like I can't quite remember. Like when you study for a test and then when you go to write an answer down, the answer just barely stays out of your memory. It's driving me crazy . . .

like a word on the tip of my tongue, something about this is on the tip of my understanding."

"Ok," Alec decided to mess with her a little. "What if you suddenly know that there is a creature that abducts city officials . . . do you get a search party together?"

Lila took the question seriously "It depends on the motive of the creature."

Alec laughed. "You would want to protect people, wouldn't you?"

"Again, it depends on the whole story." Lila was quiet for a moment, and then continued on seriously. "When I was in 2nd grade I had a friend named Bruce. Every morning I would eat breakfast & lunch at school, because my parents both had to be at work early. Bruce was always in the lunchroom during breakfast too, but he didn't get a meal. He just had to get dropped off early. When the bell rang, kids packed up and headed to their rooms and the lunch ladies started cleaning up the breakfast bar. I move a little slow in the mornings, so I was always still packing up as the room was about empty. I noticed that Bruce would walk past the breakfast bar and grab a banana or granola bar or something almost every day, and he would stick it in his pocket. At first, I was going to tell on him. But, I watched and saw that Bruce ate for lunch whatever he stole each morning. I was a little curious because I knew, even at that age, that schools provided lunch to kids who couldn't afford them. So, I wasn't sure why Bruce was stealing. One day I asked straight out if he got a free lunch or if he paid. Bruce got really mad and said his parents would *never* ask for handouts or free lunches. Then I noticed, for the first time at that age, that Bruce's clothes were pretty dirty and he borrowed a lot of school supplies from other kids. I decided that he needed the food he stole. He was eating it, not wasting it. So, I didn't say anything. Actually, I started helping. If Bruce wasn't able to grab something—I did it for him a few times. I gave him the banana or granola. He never said anything about it and neither did I. What we didn't know was that over Christmas break that year, the school got cameras installed. Two weeks after Christmas break, Bruce and I got called to the principals office to find our parents there. We had been caught taking breakfast stuff on the camera. Bruce's parents said that I probably taught him to steal . . . sort of a "thieving Indian" sterotype . . . of course that was just the sort of thing that made my parents ignore our heritage . . . the negative sterotypes. Bruce didn't correct them. I think he was too embarrassed to admit he stole because his parents didn't have the money for lunch and were too proud for free lunches. I never said anything because I decided it was not my secret to tell. It wasn't easy to not defend myself, but it was the right thing to do. So, if a creature has a good reason for abducting city officials, it may just not be my place to stop him." Now Lila smiled. Although she was joking about the hypothetical creature, Alec knew the story from 2nd grade was true. Not all answers are simple, and he was glad that she had such a strong character.

"You sure are full of life stories." He smiled at her as they got back in the car.

As they made their way back to Alec's house, he got a text from his dad. "*I'm ok—don't tell anyone I'm missing, I'll contact you soon.*"

CHAPTER 11

Alec spent the next two days helping his mom around the house while making calls to Lila. He had tried calling and texting Chet back, with no luck. As Alec was sweeping up the back porch, he sat down and looked at the yard behind his mom's home. The yard swept up into a kind of wavy hill that was bordered by a wooded area. Alec loved that hill—every winter he spent hours sled riding down it. He had some distant memories of Chet sledding with him many years ago, back before the divorce. Thinking of Chet brought Alec back to the present. It was really out of character for his dad to leave cryptic messages, and Alec was beginning to get really worried.

Finally, after lunch Lila called and told him to come to Sam's as soon as he could. With a little excuse making, Alec was able to get out of the rest of the housework until later.

Alec sped to Sam's house to find Lila, Sam and Brooks waiting. "Ok, we may be getting somewhere," smiled Sam, "you better sit down . . . this may take awhile." Sam had thrown himself into this project and researched like a crazy man. He got Brooks in on it also, which was helpful since Brooks already knew legends and history.

"This is what I found out," started Sam. "Around 1000 B.C. the Adena people lived in the Ohio River valley. According to what we know through history, these people were reported to have had a massive bone structure . . . they were big people. They were also known as the people responsible for the mound building in Ohio."

"Like the Serpent mounds?" asked Alec.

"Right" replied Sam. "At about the same time in history, there is a little bit of information known about another tribe of people called the Ronnongwetowanca. These people were described as giants and were said to inhabit vast areas, so they would be found in a lot of areas in America, I guess. Legends were passed along through Indian tribes about why the Great Spirit would create these people. In the history of the Native American people, the Ronnongwetowanca people were said to have been a vicious group who attacked often. And what we have been led to believe is that other tribes banded together and killed all of the Ronnongwetowanca throughout all the lands. However, after talking to Uncle Brooks, it seems that true legends describe a totally different scenario. The Ronnongwetowanca were actually created by the Great Spirit to protect people who honored the forest. The word Ronnongwetowanca is broken down to mean "quiet spirit watchers."

Sam took a breath and continued. "As fur traders and explorers came to what is now Ohio, the native people at that time knew that the spirit watchers needed to be protected. So, they started the story about the Ronnongwetowanca being all killed off. In truth, this race of people flourished and spread. Maybe even spread around the world."

"So are you inferring that I hit a Ronnongwetowanca person with my truck?" Lila asked incrediously "And why wouldn't any of these people have been seen before?"

"Well," continued Sam, "people today are easily misled because there is a myth that no bones or remains of these giant people exist. But, they have existed right under our noses all through history! You see, mound building sites in Ohio alone top over ten thousand locations. At this point in history, many of these sites have been leveled and built upon leaving very few untouched today."

"My dad said that the mounds were the key." Alec started putting pieces together in his mind "He *knew*, or he knows about all of this!"

"Probably" Sam said excitedly. "Zoning officials have to know some of the true history . . . I looked up some more recent history on this subject and it seems that in the early 1800's, remains of this giant race of spirit watchers began to emerge as people populated this area and built on ancient burial sites. I found this on the internet . . ." Sam handed a print out to Alec.

Alec read aloud, "*In 1829, giant human skeletons were found in a mound in Chesterville.*" He continued to the next paragraph. "*In 1872, the same type of skeletons were found in a mound in Seneca Township. More were found in 1878 in Ashtabula.*"

Sam jumped in, "From what I read, these are just a few examples—remains . . . bones and stuff . . . have been found in nearly every major mound site in Ohio during excavation. But only a few details, such as dates, are known because this information has been passed along verbally . . . through stories. I asked Brooks about this and he told me that one reason that the government is involved in zoning building sites, is to watch for potential *liabilities* that could disrupt the history that they have made up and want us to believe. A bunch of mound sites had been intentionally destroyed by the government, before the land was sold to people. But some were overlooked, and that is how other people have seen proof of the giants."

"Wow," said Lila "You have really been busy figuring this out . . . but where have all the bones and whatever else was found in the mounds gone?"

Sam shook his head, "What Brooks and I figured is that remains were either destroyed or kept by the government. When I looked up where to find archaeological discoveries in Ohio, I was referred to the Smithsonian museum in Washington D.C. The Smithsonian has tons of artifacts that are sealed away and virtually inaccessible to everyone except a select few. Ohio mound artifacts are mainly categorized under 'items under research'—no information is given under the excuse that research is being done. But some of these things were found 200 years ago . . . how stinking long does it take to research an item?"

"So if this relates to my dad," said Alec "do you think he's seen any of this?"

Sam continued on, "I'm not sure, but from what I've read, it seems like even government workers in the 1800's didn't have much of a clue *what* they were hiding and why. But, in the past few decades, people in general have become more curious about the government and about what we don't know . . . so more questions have been asked. In the past 50 years, 37 zoning workers have been in auto accidents or have just come up missing. I really don't know much about statistics, but that seems like a high number to just be coincidence. Alec, from what you've said about your grandfather . . ."

"Whoa," said Alec "you now think the government did away with my grandpa because he was a curious zoning inspector? This is getting a little far-fetched for me . . . he was just in an accident . . . it happens every day."

"That could very well be the case." replied Sam. "Just hear me out. When your grandfather died, no one went through his boxes of paperwork until last week when your dad finally found the time. Then suddenly, your dad goes missing. And you find a zoning report book with pages ripped out and the scrap leading to the newspaper article. Maybe they both figured out something that was worth keeping secret."

Thoughtfully, Alec rolled this over in his mind. "But, why don't the Native Americans just tell their side of the story and let everyone know about these giant people? Are they afraid that he government will come in & kill *them* all?"

Sam peered intensely at Alec, "In a way, that's already been done."

***Some information in Chapter 11, along with italicized sections, were taken from Giants of Ohio (see references).

CHAPTER 12

Alec balked at Sam's response about Native American's being afraid of the government. "Has there been a recent Indian massacre that I've missed?"

"No, no," replied Sam "what I mean is, the government silenced the red men a long time ago by moving them out and taking their land. The Native American tribes protected their giant brothers by remaining silent . . . that allowed the giant spirit watchers to stay in this area and watch over the land without the white men knowing. But when documented findings began to be recorded in the early 1800's, this set in motion a historical revolution of sorts. It was a catalyst that let white people know that spirit watchers were here . . . red men could not compete with the guns and power of the white men taking over the land, but one silent tribe stayed and protected the forests. As Brooks and I pieced together this whole thing, we tried to think from every angle. It was not just about power & land . . . it was about white men making money. Think about it . . . if you were a European settler coming to America to prosper and be free, would you want to move to an area populated with giant savage men? Heck no!" Sam answered himself.

"There are enough mythical creatures in Europe . . . the loch ness monster, werewolves, and other stuff . . . no one would leave the east coast to come to a forest full of giants! So, the government put the squeeze on Indians to stop the legends. There were already battles over land by that time; industry was coming to Ohio and I'm sure it was easy to push out any remaining regular tribes that were still here protecting the giants. Without legends to tell about them, they were "dead" to people here."

Brooks stepped up behind Sam "You're doing a good job at filling them in," he smiled.

Alec looked at Sam then Brooks "But I'm still not getting the point of pushing out the last tribes if giant remains were already found."

Brooks nodded "Too many things were happening at once . . . the Delaware tribe gave up the last of their land in Ohio during the same year as the first remains were found. The Wyandot seemed to have the strongest link with the giants . . . maybe because of their strong beliefs in passing down Native American culture. But, even they were pushed out by 1842, marking the end of organized tribal life in Ohio."

Sam cut in, "Leaving no tribes to pass down legends and no tribes to look out for the giants."

Alec sighed, looking overwhelmed with all that has been explained. "Even if all of your theories are true . . . I don't have any proof, and how can any of this help me find my dad? Besides, what does it matter at this point? If these giant spirit watchers have been hidden for all of these years, what's the point in outing them now?"

Lila looked at Alec and quietly responded, "Alec, you wanted to know the truth about the black cow and you want to know what is going on with your dad and with your grandfather's death. If this stuff is true, isn't it fair to let everyone know? Besides, Native Americans have been badly mistreated . . . let's let people know how they stood by and protected their legend and their spirit watchers . . . and maybe let people know that spirit watchers are still here protecting the land that was taken from all red people."

Alec nodded, but replied, "We still have no proof."

Lila looked over at Brooks, "As Chief Manitou, you've heard and told tons of Indian legends . . ."

Sam responded, gesturing toward Brooks "Brooks said that he's known about spirit watcher since he was a boy, but he rarely tells those legends. Over the years, people have formed ideas in their minds from television and bizarre stories. Legends of spirit watcher can easily end up becoming corny Bigfoot myths with white people."

"But why do they take real legends and discredit them?" Lila puzzled.

"Simple," Brooks stepped in, "there is no better way to hide the truth than to discredit it. By making spirit watchers a joke, no one wants to be involved . . . or else *they* may become the butt of jokes. If no one talks about the giants, settlers move in, industry grows . . . people make money."

"There has to be something else involved," Alec jumped in, "my dad wouldn't go off without something concrete to back up all of this. We went through all of the papers at the house, I checked his office . . . ," Then the piece fell into place with Alec. "My Aunt Char!"

Lila looked confused "What does your aunt have to do with this?"

Alec was excited now, "My dad said that he was mailing a package to my Aunt Char during our last phone conversation . . . why would he tell me about his errands unless he needed me to know?" Alec didn't finish his thought. He looked at Sam and Lila, "Let's go on a little road trip."

CHAPTER 13

A lec, Lila and Sam piled into Alec's Jeep.
"My aunt lives in New Philadelphia, so we can get there in an hour or less," Alec told the other two. The jeep sped down Interstate 77, then east down Route 39. At the center of town in New Philadelphia, Alec took a left. His aunt lived across from Tuscora Park and this was a Friday in summer. Traffic was busy with parents hauling small kids to enjoy the rides and swimming before the end of summer. Alec pulled into the driveway of his aunt's home and the trio hopped out of the Jeep. Knowing her house was empty, Alec went directly to the garage where he knew she kept her spare house key. Aunt Char worked with a bunch of animal activist groups and spent a lot of time traveling to different events. When she was younger she traveled around the world helping different areas set up refuge areas for endangered species. But now, she stays in the states mostly, working on making people aware of wildlife issues and making sure animals needing protection get protected. She had been really glad when Alec got a job at the parks for the summer and thought it was a step toward helping wildlife, even though he really didn't get a chance to do much with animals. He grabbed the key

and nearly collided with the neighbor, Mrs. Pattison, as he turned back around.

"Oh Alec!" she exclaimed "I haven't seen you in ages! I wasn't expecting any visitors here at your aunt's house since she's away now," she looked at Alec questioningly.

Alec stammered, "Oh—well, we just came to Tuscora Park for lunch and I though I'd check on the house for her . . . we were down this way doing some exploring anyway."

"How nice!" Mrs. Pattison seemed content with his explanation. "Just lock up when you leave. I've been watering plants and bringing in her mail."

"Great" replied Alec, "you have a good day Mrs. Pattison."

She smiled and walked back next door as Sam and Lila approached. They went to the side door and Lila gave Alec a hopeful look as they approached. The trio entered Aunt Char's kitchen. There was a laundry basket on the old country table and it was already overflowing with mail.

Alec took only a few minutes to shuffle through and find an envelope with a return address from his dad.

"This seems way too thin to have any amount of information in it." Alec held the envelope doubtfully. "But there is a lump in it . . ."

"Let's take it and go," said Lila, "there isn't any other mail from your dad here, so this must be it." The group locked up Aunt Char's house, returned the spare key and climbed back into Alec's Jeep. Sam drove so that Alec could open the envelope. As he tore it open a brass key fell out onto his lap. Alec pulled out a business card and a scrap of paper. The card was for First Citizens Bank in Alliance and the number 715 was on the back. The brass key also had the number 715 inscribed on it.

"That has to be for a safety deposit box." Lila said, "What's on the other paper?"

The scrap of paper simply said:

> *Char—Please hold on to this for me. The mounds are the real key just like dad had written in his journal. See you soon-Chet*

Alec smiled. "Whatever is in this lock box really is information about the giant people, I think."

Lila hugged Alec's arm as a chill went through her. "But how do we get in that lock box and what do we do then?"

CHAPTER 14

lec, Lila and Sam headed back to Stark County, formulating a plan on the way. The only way to get to a lock box is to sign for it with the bank teller. Alec had never been a sneaky kid, so the idea of forging his dad's signature to get in the lock-box was unsettling. By the time they got back, there wasn't time to go to the bank before closing. They drove back to Sam's house and Alec then headed to his mom's house for the night.

In the morning, Sam and Lila picked Alec up and headed to the bank. In the car, he practiced signing what he thought looked like his dad's signature. Trying to get to the lock box himself was the best plan that they could come up with.

At First Citizen Bank, Alec looked anxiously at Lila and Sam. "Wish me luck," he said as he slowly got out of the vehicle. If the cashiers asked for identification, Alec's plan would tank. But, he had to try to see what was in that box.

Alec approached the counter and a smiling red-headed lady greeted him, "Good afternoon, how can I help you?"

Alec smiled back and set the key on the counter. "Hi. I need to get in my lock-box . . . number 715 . . . please."

"Sure thing," said the woman as she took the key and went to a file. She came back carrying a paper and a matching key.

"Ok, I need to see your identification and I will need your signature."

Crap. So much for his great plan.

She continued, "Are you Chester or Alestair? I assume you are not Charlotte."

Alec looked at her dumbfounded. Chet had put him on the card to have access to the box. This box that he never knew about.

Alec regained his composure and replied, "Uh, I'm Alec . . . Alestair."

"Well then," she continued "this is your first time here, so I'll need to make a copy of your driver's license while you sign."

Alec gave the red-headed lady his driver's license, signed the entry sheet and followed her back to the vault. Each box required two keys to open it. He had one and she had one. They pulled out box 715 and the red-headed lady showed him a table that he could sit at to look through it before she left.

Alec took a deep breath and opened the box. Inside was an envelope with his birth certificate, his dad's birth certificate, a marriage certificate from his parents and their divorce paperwork. There were some other papers attached with Chet's retirement information, a 401K plan and investment information was written down. Ok, this was boring . . . where is the information he needed? He looked through a jewelry box that contained a few rings that Alec assumed had belonged to his grandmother. The only other thing there was an old composition notebook. It had the standard black and white cover and the corners were worn, showing that this was a well-used notebook. Alec opened the front and saw sketches of what he assumed were land plots at various angles. Ok, zoning people had professional land sketches . . . why was this filled with clearly non-professional drawings on lined paper? As Alec flipped through the notebook, he saw scribbled writing on some pages and on the back of the cover with the initials HD. Henry DeWalt. This must be his grandpa's "journal". If this were a movie, the journal would have been some old thick book bound in crafted leather, maybe with some dust on top that he could blow off. But, this was real life and his big clue was an old composition notebook that smelled slightly of . . . coffee. Alec sniffed the back where an old stain had set in. Well, it was something. He put the box back and signed out with the red-headed lady, taking the notebook with him.

When Alec got back to the car, he handed the notebook to Lila as Sam drove. The three went back to Sam's house and looked through the journal. The drawings seemed very encrypted to Alec, but they probably made sense to Grandpa Henry. It was hard to tell what he was thinking, or what his point was in the sketches and vague notes. There were a lot of notes about mounds, soil levels, and distances. Some of the sketches were of land how it would look if you were standing in front of it and some were from an overhead view. The first break through came about half way through the notebook. There was a drawing of a farm area showing a small mound. In the margin was written:

Rebillot farm—Meese

"Hey!" Alec exclaimed, "I know where that is!" Meese was a road on the outskirts of Louisville and the barn had one of those roofs with the family name written on it in different colored shingles. Meese was a back road that Alec sometimes took and the name Rebillot was unusual enough that it stuck out in his mind. The group decided to visit the site after they went through the rest of the notebook.

The next, and only other, clue was at the very end of the notebook. There were two sketches, professional ones that were stuffed into the notebook. One was of an area that looked like farm land, or at least it was farm land when the sketch was drawn. The other had a grid like an allotment with some landform drawings along the side. Both seemed familiar to Alec, but he could not put his finger on why.

CHAPTER 15

Alec didn't know what to make of the sketches at the end of the notebook, so he put that clue on the back burner for now.

Sam had to go to work, so Alec and Lila set out together to look at the Rebillot farm. They drove Alec's Jeep down Meese Road noticing that the road had areas surrounded by cornfield, much like Parks Road.

When they came to the farm with the old barn having the Rebillot name on it, they stopped. "What should we do?" Alec asked, suddenly unsure of how to proceed.

Lila flashed her smile as her green eyes lit up "Let's go connect some dots to our puzzle!"

☆　☆　☆

At the door to the run down farmhouse, Alec knocked. A lady who looked a little older than Chet answered the door. She did not smile, but looked curiously at Lila and Alec.

"What do you kids want?' she demanded.

Alec was starting to feel sorry he had come here "Uh, Mrs. Rebillot?"

"No" she snapped.

"Well, uh, we are, um, we have some questions about the Rebillot farm and . . ." she cut Alec off.

"I really don't have time for answering questions that aren't your business. So, if you'll just find your way off my property . . ."

A voice from behind her piped up shakily "Barbara, it's still *my* property . . . who's at the door?"

The woman was clearly annoyed.

"Just some kids, dad." She tried to start closing the door when the voice continued.

"Well, let them in!"

The woman, who must be Barbara, rolled her eyes and opened the screen door to let Alec and Lila into the shabby living room.

"This is my father, Frank Rebillot."

"I thought you said that this isn't the Rebillot farm?" Alec asked.

"No," said the woman "I said that *I* am not Mrs. Rebillot. That was my Momma. Dad, I'm going back in the kitchen. Let these kids out when you're done talking." Barbara turned and left without another glance at Lila or Alec.

The duo turned to look at the elderly man in the recliner. The room was suddenly more pleasant with only the man and two kids.

"Thank you for talking to us Mr. Rebillot" Alec began.

"I'm Frank and it's good to have some young people to talk to" the man smiled, "sit down please and tell me what brings you here."

Not wanting to tell this nice man their whole crazy story, Lila turned on her charm and told Frank that they were doing a school report on zoning and land features in their community. Fortunately, Frank didn't ask why they were doing a report in August and what teacher would assign a zoning report.

"Well, I'm not sure how much I can help you, but I'll answer any questions you have."

Alec and Lila asked about when the farm was built and land features that were on the land. They hedged into the topic of mounds.

"Was the ground level or did they need to, um, flatten any areas when this was built?"

"The farm was built by my grandpa," said Frank. "I don't rightly know how level it was. But when I added the building to house a generator, I needed to have a zoning person come out before leveling some land."

"When was that?" Alec asked anxiously.

"Oh, about 15 years ago. Right before my son-in-law took over running the farm."

"What happened with that?" Lila pressed.

"Nothing really," Frank replied "the zoning people were really nice—checked out the land and even had some of their own people come level it for me. Hauled away the dirt and everything."

Lila and Alec looked at each other. Alec knew enough about zoning to know that zoning people didn't excavate and haul away dirt. Lila must have sensed his energy or seen his aura, because her eyes widened. The couple thanked Frank for his time and kindness as they made their way to the door.

Suddenly, Lila turned and asked, "Frank? Since you have lived in this area for a long time, can you tell me . . . do cows get loose often?"

Frank looked at her curiously, "I guess one gets out now and then, but not usually."

"Are black cows somehow more likely to get loose than, you know, other cows?"

Frank's face suddenly clouded over. "Why are you kids really here?" he demanded in a shaky voice.

CHAPTER 16

Alec and Lila looked startled.

"I didn't mean to upset you," Lila said "it's just that my car hit a black cow not far from here."

"Did you see it?" Frank looked at her with full attention.

"Not really" Lila sat back down next to Frank. "Actually, I don't think it was a cow, but that's what the police told me it was."

Frank brought his thin hand up to his chin thoughtfully and shook his head. Alec sat back down too.

"I guess I'm old enough now that it doesn't matter if people think I'm crazy." Frank mumbled half to himself. He looked up "I've always been a farmer, but when I was young I also worked part time for the local police department, to make some extra money and to help the community. Anyway, most all farmers know that there are animals that roam the land and we don't always get a good view of them. That's kind of what a black cow is."

Lila looked confused "So, a black cow isn't really a cow?"

"No, it sure isn't" replied Frank. "We don't talk about what black cows really are. Best thing I can compare it to is what people call a Bigfoot. My kids were growing up in the 1970's and there was this movie about Bigfoot out . . .

everyone poked fun at people who started believing it was real. But anyone who has spent time on land or in the woods knows that there are creatures that are big. They keep to themselves. Don't hurt crops or livestock. Actually, it's rare to see one. But you spend enough time out, you'll catch a glimpse. Anyway, police who grew up in back areas like this knew, and still know, that these creatures roam about too. But, no one wants to be pegged as a crazy, so farmers and some law people use the term 'black cow' instead. Every now and then one of them gets hit by a car or gets accidently hurt during hunting season or something . . . and if they need to be . . . talked about . . . we call them black cows."

☆   ☆   ☆

After thanking Frank profusely again, Lila and Alec rushed out to the Jeep.

"Your Uncle Brooks was right" Alec said. "The giants . . . mound builders . . . spirit watchers."

"Dots are connecting," Lila said with a smile.

"Yeah," replied Alec. "Except the dot that tells me where my dad is."

CHAPTER 17

A lec & Lila went back to Alec's mom's house to sort through all the new information and see how it could lead them to Chet.

They determined that spirit watchers, a.k.a. *Black cows*, were real and that they buried their dead in mounds that the government does not want people to know about. Lila's truck hit one and the police lied about what it was. And Alec's dad had this notebook of information and could now not be reached. Alec walked back to his favorite hill and lied down. He looked up into the sky then closed his eyes, wondering what to do with what he now knew.

☆　☆　☆

The rest of the weekend was pretty uneventful. Lila and Alec both had their own things to do at home and both spent time pondering what to do next. The last time Alec had heard from his dad, Chet told him not to tell anyone he was missing, So Alec stayed quiet—for now.

On Monday morning, Alec tried Chet's cell phone for about the fiftieth time, and Chet answered.

"Dad!" Alec exclaimed "Where are you?"

"It's fine son, I'm fine," said Chet calmly. "Just hold tight. I'm still working with a few people on some old matters."

"I know about the mounds, Dad. And I think I know . . . well, other stuff too." Alec didn't want to blurt out all that he and Lila had discovered right away.

Chet sighed, "I was afraid that you would figure it out and get dragged into this. Listen, I'll call you soon. I just wanted to let you know not to worry. Love you Al." With that, Chet hung up.

Alec was bewildered, but at least not so worried anymore. He called Lila to tell her that his dad was ok, although still M.I.A. After listening to his good news, Lila told him that she had just left the library. "JoAnn found an article that she thought might go along with what you want and she copied it. I told her I would get it to you."

"Great!" said Alec, genuinely glad that he would have a pressing reason to see Lila. "Can we meet now?"

Lila laughed, "If you had my freakish ability, you would know that I'm on my way to your house now."

CHAPTER 18

Gina was at work today, so Alec and Lila could sit in the kitchen and talk about the little mystery that they were involved with.

"Here we go," said Lila as she pulled out a paper from her bag, "fresh from JoAnn."

The article was from the Stark County Farm Bureau. Apparently, the county library kept records of local publications other than just newspapers.

The article was about a farmer who wanted to buy some wooded area adjacent to his field, and then timber it. It was government land spanning 50 acres and it was surrounded by the back sides of various farm fields. The farmer was complaining because he wanted to expand his field and the government wouldn't sell the land because it was listed as a protected wildlife habitat. It was not zoned for personal or commercial use. When the farmer in question got a petition signed to change the zoning because *"the only wildlife on that land is skunks, groundhogs and a few deer."*, the Native American council stepped in. After a meeting with the council and zoning, the issue was dropped.

"Well," said Alec, "this does fall under the category of Native American and construction, I guess. I wonder if there are mounds on this land?"

"I don't know" replied Lila taking the paper back. "I'll hold on to it for now."

☆   ☆   ☆

Alec and Lila made some lunch and continued talking for the next hour or so when Lila's green eyes sparkled and she jumped up "I don't know why we are sitting here wondering aimlessly . . . Uncle Brooks is involved with the Native American Council . . . let's just ask if he knows anything about this."

Lila made a few calls and found that her uncle was in Ashtabula. She finally got him on the phone and read the farm bureau article to him. "Do you know anything about this?"

Brooks replied thoughtfully, "Yes. I know that area and the situation." After a pause he added "I also have a pretty good idea where Alec's dad is."

CHAPTER 19

Alec set a time to meet Brooks at Sam's house. Brooks clearly didn't want to talk any more about this situation on the phone.

Alec & Lila continued to talk about what they had found out, and each interjected a little flirting into the conversation as well. Lila was one of those people that Alec felt like he could really talk to and he could be himself with her. Before either of them knew it, Alec's mom came in from work. Gina was happy to see Alec and always loved to see him bring friends over. She was making chit-chat with Lila when she spotted the composition notebook.

"Oh my goodness! Is that your Grandpa Henry's old journal?" Gina exclaimed.

Alec was surprised, "Yeah mom. But, why would you know that?"

Gina smiled, "Henry carried that everywhere with him—he was a good man . . . and he just adored you, Alec. He always had this journal with little zoning sketches in it. He was dedicated to his job . . . just like your dad."

"Do you know why he wanted to make his own personal zoning notes?" Alec continued.

"I don't know," Gina said, "but he would see an area and sketch away with his mind in his own world. In fact, one time right before he died, he was sitting in the back watching you play and he started sketching and scribbling like crazy. He was so absorbed that when I brought him a cup of coffee, he bumped it and it spilled all over the back."

Alec remembered the stain and turned over the notebook. Gina smiled "That's it. He shook off the coffee and kept working. There was something about the hill you were playing on that had him thinking. I guess zoning people are always thinking of working around landforms when new allotments pop up."

Alec thought of the sketch of an allotment in the notebook. That's' why it looked familiar. It was the allotment where his mom lived.

"Why would he care about your back yard?" Lila interjected now.

"Oh, the field and woods behind us was going to be developed too, sweetie." Gina smiled, "It never happened, which was good for us. Alec loved having that hill in the back and the woods gave us privacy . . . better than more houses to look at."

A thought coursed through Alec like a current of electricity—his hill . . . was a mound. Maybe. Why else would Grandpa Henry be so interested?

Lila and Alec looked at each other with new clarity again that day. "Interesting," said Alec. "Well mom, we have to go—I'm taking Lila to her brother's house."

Gina looked disappointed that the kids weren't staying. But Alec and Lila were in a hurry to get to Sam's house. Brooks would be there soon.

CHAPTER 20

S am was just getting home from work when Alec and Lila arrived. He greeted them with a wave and a smile. "Well, how goes the mystery?" Lila and Alec filled Sam in on all the new information before Brooks arrived. When Brooks finally pulled in and joined the trio on Sam's porch, Alec was all but bursting with anticipation.

"Well?" said Lila.

Brooks cut straight to the chase. "You know that I am on the Native American Council for this area . . . well the council head contacted the rest of us today about a situation developing over some land. Someone found out about a plot of wildlife sanctuary land protected by the Native Americans. Apparently a zoning official was asking questions and some lady stepped in . . . anyway there is a dispute about this land and what should be done."

"And you think the zoning guy is my dad?" asked Alec.

"I think so," said Brooks, "I made the connection when Lila said she was with you in Louisville. The plot of land is in Louisville."

"Well, my dad would get involved with land in the town where I grew up if there was a problem, I guess. But why the secrecy? And why is the Native American Council involved?" said Alec.

Brooks sighed. "The council watches over certain plots of land for wildlife."

Alec persisted "Why wouldn't the Ohio Department of Wildlife cover that? There are no Indian reservations in Ohio . . . I know from history class that wild game and farming were good here and white men pushed out Native Americans and set up their own trade with canals and stuff."

"That's very true," said Brooks. "But some wildlife is still under Native American protection . . . the spirit watchers."

"You've known more about all of this the whole time!" cried Lila. "How could you make Alec worry?"

"Wait," said Brooks, "I pointed Sam in the right direction by relaying the history of the Ronnongwetowanca. I'm sworn by the council to help protect our spirit watchers, so I don't talk about them to anyone outside the council. Not even my family."

"But your telling us now," said Alec. "And I'm not a Native American."

"Yes. But you're worried about your dad and I think you kids would figure this out on your own soon anyway." said Brooks "I heard that you are checking old articles about natives and land."

"Uncle Brooks!" said Lila, "How exactly do you know what we've been doing?"

"I don't know everything, but I *am* friends with JoAnn . . . remember?" Brooks responded.

Lila and Alec nodded together. "So where is my dad at exactly?" Alec got back on track.

"There is a government office that is secured and used for situations like this. That's where the zoning guy . . . probably your dad . . . and the wildlife lady are at."

"Situations like this?" Sam inquired.

Brooks gave a quick nod, "More classified situations occur than you would want to know about."

"Let's just deal with *this* situation for now," pressed Lila, "Where are we going?"

"We aren't going anywhere" said Brooks, "the situation is a problem because the zoning guy found information on a particular plot of land and he went right to the top to see about changing the zoning to residential rather than wildlife sanctuary. The lady is a representative of some wildlife group and I don't know if she really even knows what type of sanctuary this is, but she wants it preserved."

"How would a wildlife group know about people talking about a zoning change and why would my dad try to take away land from these alleged spirit watchers?"

Brooks had his chin in his hands thoughtfully, "Alec, can you take me to your mom's home?"

CHAPTER 21

After determining that Gina would ask way too many questions, the group formulated a plan. Lila and Alec would drive in one vehicle while Brooks and Sam followed in another. Lila would ask Gina to come with her to the mall to help pick out an outfit. Never having a daughter, Gina jumped at any opportunity to play "mom" with a girl. Alec was not a shopper and Gina was a shopaholic . . . so the group felt confident in this plan.

Sam and Brooks watched the two younger people walk into Alec's home in Louisville. Sure as anything, within 10 minutes Gina and Lila walked out with Gina carrying her purse and chattering away. It was already seven-thirty and the mall closed at nine, so Alec knew that Gina couldn't keep Lila shopping for too long.

When the girls drove away, Sam and Brooks got out of Sam's car and headed toward the house.

Alec let Sam and Brooks in, then the trio went through to the back yard. Brooks looked at the hill behind the house as he stepped outside. It really looked just like any other normal slope that might be found anywhere. Brooks climbed up the side while Alec and Sam followed. He walked around the top, looking down, then up and down again. The top of the hill was fairly flat and was around 3 feet wide and maybe 12 feet long. It sloped back down on all sides, with the side away from the house covered with some trees and brush, leading into a wooded area. On the top, one side was a little wider than the other—about three and a half feet graduating down to three feet. It did not look perfect or man made. But to Broooks, the sizing seemed to verify his thoughts.

"What?" asked Alec.

Brooks sighed and began "This looks like a singular effigy mound, from my experience. You see how the top is a little wider at one end? That is the head end and it is pointing toward where the sun rises on the summer solstice. Ancient people lived their lives by the sky, so burial direction had real meaning to them. And the size is right . . . and most important, this is at the edge of a preserved area."

That was a bomb that dropped on Alec heavily. "Preserved area?" Alec said with disbelief, "Do you mean that right behind my house, where I played as a kid for years, there are spirit watchers?"

Brooks replied steadily, "This is a plot of land intended for their use, but they mostly roam where they want."

"Then why have any preserves at all . . . if they go wherever they want?" Sam now questioned.

Brooks continued, "As people, we roam . . . to work, to play, to wherever we need to go. But we have safe places, like home, for times when we need to be safe and protected. The preserves around the state . . . and country for that matter . . . give the spirit watchers a safe place. When they are sick, injured or when they are having and raising their young. Alec, you probably never even saw anything or suspected. These gentle giants keep to themselves. They watch the land, but they don't want to be seen or bothered by us. That is why the Native American Council still protects them. It is our heritage, what our ancestors have taught us to do, and what we will teach our children and grandchildren to do."

Alec and Sam both soaked in what Brooks was saying. Like any other living creature, the giant spirit watchers needed a habitat.

As Alec pondered, he asked, "Why don't Native Americans just tell the world about them now? I understand that years ago the white people wanted to settle the area and not freak people out with giants. But what about now? People have lived near spirit watchers for generations without even knowing, so if they know now . . . maybe people will be OK with it and all this secret stuff won't need to go on."

Brooks gave a little smile. "Maybe. But there are a few things to think about. Some people still will be 'freaked out'. Also, men can be cruel and stupid. Of course there would be people who would want to break on to preserved areas to get pictures and some people would be interested in them because of they are different and strange. But also scientists would be cruel, unintentionally. They would want to study the spirit watchers and dissect their bodies when they died. These creatures are solitary . . . their souls have been hurt by people massacuring the land and living around them in an unpeaceful way. When they have finished their lives here on Earth, they want to continue to be solitary and be in peace. Having people follow them, maybe try to cage them and unearth their bodies to find out more . . . that could crush what remains of their race." Brooks sighed again, "Men have taken over so much . . . the land, pushed out wildlife and it seems like some need to have control over everything. Can't we just leave the spirit watchers alone? They are one last reminder of what this area was once about." Brooks was visibly upset, so Sam jumped in, "Ok, Ok . . . we get it. Let's go now and leave Alec to think about all this before his mom comes back."

Alec wasn't really sure if he 'got it', but he did need some time to himself. He walked Sam and Brooks to the front and made plans to meet them first thing in the morning. Brooks was going to take him to see if the zoning guy in question was actually his dad.

When Gina and Lila returned, Alec took Lila to the back yard and gave her a quick recap of what Brooks said. Lila was as astonished as Alec had been.

"I don't know, Alec," said Lila, "I think people are smart enough to help the spirit watchers . . . keeping secrets from the world just seems wrong."

"I know," said Alec. "Maybe this is our chance to really connect some dots for the world. If there is someone from the press around and we tell them about all of this, then people will start to know and learn about spirit watchers."

Lila smiled "I'll make some calls tonight." Then she said her goodbyes and dashed out the door.

☆   ☆   ☆

Alec went back outside after Gina had gone up to bed. He thought about his dad and his grandpa Henry . . . who had maybe given his life because of keeping spirit watcher secrets. He thought of how Lila wasn't close with her parents because they thought Native American stories made their people look foolish. This could be big. Really big. Let the truth come out, then his dad won't have to be gone to protect any secret places and Brooks won't have to keep things from Sam and Lila. Yes, this would be big, and a good thing.

Alec stood up and as he turned, something in the tree line caught his eye. For a slight moment, he saw a face of something . . . no some *one*. It walked between two trees and the moonlight lit up the space where it moved. A face, surrounded by hair but with the features of a person. It . . . no *he* . . . didn't look sad, as much as sort of disappointed. For that very brief moment, Alec met eyes with the creature and saw all the wisdom and pain in hundreds of years of people. It was a look of knowing and fatigue . . . like someone who has been at work for a very long day and is now very tired. The intelligence and wisdom shone bright in those eyes, and then the face was gone.

Alec blinked and looked hard again at the tree line. Did he really just see someone there?

"Hello?" he called as he walked, then trotted up his hill. He got to the spot where he saw the eyes. The wooded area behind the tree line was black with the darkness of night, and completely silent. No crickets or owls . . . no sound at all. Alec got a strange and uneasy feeling, then backed away back to the porch. He kept his eyes on the tree line as he walked in the back door and firmly locked the bolt.

CHAPTER 22

"Where is your father?" That was the first thing Alec heard when he woke up the next morning.

"What?" he replied groggily as Gina sat looking at him on his bed.

"I've been trying for a couple days to get a hold of your dad . . . so that we could set up a little farewell party for you before you left for college. But, he hasn't returned any calls and you haven't been over to his house all week. Chet never is this irresponsible about calling back, so where is he?" Gina asked again.

"I'll get a hold of him today and have him call you," Alec replied and secretly hoped that he could follow up on his promise. "Right now, I have to get up and going."

"You've been 'off and going' a lot for a kid who doesn't have school or a job at the moment." Gina was suspicious now.

Alec gave her a quick peck on the cheek, "Don't worry Mom, I'll spend more time with you before I leave. I just need to take care of a few things first."

Alec got dressed quickly and headed for Sam's house. He and Lila planned to meet there, and he called to make sure they were still on.

"We're going to meet Uncle Brooks there too and . . ." Lila stopped.

"And what?" Alec asked.

"Never mind . . . I'll talk to you when we're on our way today."

Before Alec could ask anymore, Lila said a quick goodbye and promised to meet him at Sam's house.

As expected, Sam and Brooks were at Sam's when Alec pulled in. Lila pulled in right behind him and the four stood in the front yard together.

"I'm going to take you guys to the Native American Council main building in Ashtabula. The people who have been disagreeing have been moved there so that we can settle this protected land issue."

They all piled into Alec's black Jeep and Brooks directed him along the way. Lila couldn't tell Alec whatever she was going to, but she had an odd look on her face during the drive. Alec noted that she kept looking back as they drove and he quietly kept an eye on her through the rearview mirror. The Native American Council building was as nondescript as a building could get. It was a plain brick building off West 48th Street, with a small gravel parking lot and no signs to indicated what the building was for. If Alec hadn't known better, he would have mistaken it for a warehouse building. Brooks lead them through the metal door in front and Alec noted that the corridors did have Native American photos, plaques and articles framed along the walls. Maybe Alec was expecting big headdresses or something, but the décor was very business-like. They stopped at a wooden door and Brooks open it to reveal a large conference room that had obviously been furnished twenty or thirty years ago. The room was neat and clean, but the furniture style was older and showed years of use and wear. At the table were two men that Alec did not know, along with his dad and . . . Aunt Char! Weird. Aunt Char? The lady who was interested in keeping the wildlife area preserved.

"Dad!" exclaimed Alec as he gave Chet a quick hug.

Chet smiled, "Brooks told us all that you kids had pretty much figured out what was going on. You guys will be the next generation to keep these secrets, so we decided that you should be here and give us some input."

Brooks stepped in then to introduce the two other men in the room. "This is special agent Keme and special agent Morgan. They both are government employees assigned to an off-shoot branch of the FBI. The branch in which they work deals specifically with classified information. They've overseen the preserved areas for spirit watchers for decades and now they're helping us resolve this particular issue about the preserved area in your back yard Alec."

Alec looked at his dad, "Why is this all coming up now? That land has been preserved for awhile I guess, so why now?"

Chet replied, "When I finally got some time after retiring to go through your Grandpa Henry's stuff, I found his journal. Of course I had know about these preserved areas since I was in management at the zoning office. But, they never really had anything to do with my life personally . . . until I found your grandpa's journal. I was looking through it and saw the sketch of your mom's neighborhood and I realized as I looked it over, that there was a preserved area behind the house. Al, your grandpa had that notebook with him the day he was killed in that accident . . . he knew that the area was preserved for spirit watchers."

"So where was he on his way to that day?" Alec asked.

Char cut in, "That's one thing your dad & I are disagreeing about. I think he was on his way to let the media or someone know . . . to make sure the area stayed preserved and watched over."

Chet continued, "Letting people know about spirit watchers would endanger them. I think he was on his way to try to get a preserved area somewhere else so that they wouldn't be right by you and your mom . . . but he would never go around telling people about this because it would only put the spirit watchers in the spotlight . . . and put your neighborhood in the spotlight. He was trying to get it moved."

"But if the spirit watchers aren't dangerous, why would he care?" asked Lila.

It was Brooks turn to chime in, "People are afraid of things that they don't understand—whether they are dangerous or not."

"I agree," said Chet. "Anyway, I called agent Morgan when I found the journal and headed up here to figure this out and make sure the area is safe . . ."

"And he called me," said Char, "and sent me the lock box key so that I could back him up if he needed me to. But I disagree with keeping this area secret. People would protect the spirit watchers and make sure that they are healthy. We could track them to make sure that they don't get hurt like we do with other wildlife. They must be endangered, since scientists have never 'discovered' them . . . so let's not loose them forever!"

"They've survived pretty well in spite of people taking their land, and not knowing about them up to this point." said Brooks.

Special agent Keme said, "So, that is what we are stuck on. I think we are all OK with keeping the preserved area intact . . . as long as Alec is alright with spirit watchers in the land behind him." All eyes turned to Alec as he replied "I think so . . . but first, what are you still debating?"

Chet answered, "Well, whether or not to keep this all classified. I should never have told Char, but since I did . . . now she knows and wants to make this public."

"And everyone else?" asked Sam.

"We think it is safer for everyone to keep it quiet." replied agent Morgan.

"Since Henry died with this information, I'm concerned about Char's safety if she doesn't agree . . ." added Chet.

"Mr. DeWalt," frowned agent Keme, "implying that the government would harm someone is ridiculous."

"Is it?" added Brooks. "We're hoping that you kids can talk to Char . . . I'm pretty sure that even the government wouldn't harm kids."

Agents Morgan and Keme both scowled at the remark and Alec noticed that Lila sent a quick text message and slipped her phone back in her pocket.

"I didn't want you to be involved because I wanted to keep you safe." said Chet. "But once you figured things out, I thought that total disclosure would be the best route."

"I appreciate that you trust me with this, Dad," said Alec. "I'm just not sure that keeping secrets is the best thing to do. Aunt Char has some good points . . ."

Agent Morgan looked pointedly at Alec. "Letting classified information out to the public is not an option without approval from higher up."

There was a knock on the door and Lila turned, then looked back at agent Morgan. "People always have options, and not keeping secrets is one."

She walked over and opened the door, letting in a woman who Alec recognized as a television anchor for a Cleveland network, along with a cameraman.

Lila said, "This is Samantha Davis from channel 5 and she can let all of this out."

Samantha smiled at the group, "And what a great story this will be . . . Lila was kind enough to wear a wire today, so we taped the whole thing today."

Brooks looked hurt and disappointed as he turned to Lila.

"I'm sorry if this isn't what you want, but maybe the world will understand Native Americans better, maybe zoning "accidents" won't happen and stuff that went to the Smithsonian years ago will be released for people to study . . ."

Char walked over and stood beside Lila, "Your call Alec . . . the property that brought up all this is in your backyard."

CHAPTER 23

Alec looked at Samantha Davis's gleaming eyes and then around the room at each person there. Progress and understanding comes from knowledge . . . and people can't know much if secrets are kept. He opened his mouth to respond . . . and in an instant another face flashed in his mind. The face in the trees. The tired and wise eyes. And the dots connected together for Alec.

"Ok—since this is my yard . . . will you all respect what I ask to happen?" Samantha agreed quickly, obviously confided that Alec would tell all. The others looked at each other, and then nodded slowly . . . some with more confidence than others.

Alec stepped forward and took Samantha Davis's microphone, "Samantha, this is the deal . . . you have been celebrity pranked! Seriously . . . you thought that all of this was real? Forget Punked or Candid Camera . . . we had the great idea for a new show where we prank news celebrities!"

Char and Lila looked a little confused, but the rest of the people in the room caught on pretty fast and started laughing.

"Got ya!" said Chet

Samantha was clearly not amused. "Seriously? This is just a stupid joke? I have important news stories and I don't want to look like an idiot! I know that I have to sign a release for you to air your stupid show, and I won't allow this prank to be put on television!" She turned to her camera man, who had a smirk on his face "Jim, throw out the tapes from this girl's wire." Samantha looked disgustedly at Lila, while Lila still had a blank look on her face. "As a matter of fact," said Samantha "make sure everything from today is GONE . . . I refuse to be made a fool of!" Samantha took the wire abruptly off Lila and was still giving orders to poor Jim as the two marched out of the building.

Alec turned to Char and Lila, "Lila, I know we talked about not keeping secrets, and in most circumstances that's a good philosophy. But you know from 2nd grade that there are also exceptions. Aunt Char . . . I know that you think the best of people, but try to understand that not everyone would be good to the spirit watchers. Did you two notice the look in Samantha's eyes? It was like a hungry owl going after a field mouse. She wasn't interested in preserving land for ancient people . . . she was interested in making money and making herself famous. Too many other people are like her . . . we can't risk the safety and the ways of these spirit watchers with people like that."

Lila smiled and her eyes twinkled "You're right about people like Samantha—I saw her aura this morning and almost cancelled, but I had a *freakish hunch* that you would handle this the right way."

Alec looked at Char, and Char looked disapproving at him, "Well, I don't agree. I still think that the spirit watchers should be protected by wildlife people. But Alec, I promised to respect what you decided and I don't go back on my word". Char did not look happy, but Alec knew that she would back off the issue for him.

Agent Morgan still looked concerned "Great—we all are on the same page. But how do we know that this Samantha Davis won't go and air everything at some point or keep it and let other people listen to the tape?"

Chet scoffed, "She's self centered . . . she would never risk looking like a fool."

Alec smiled and added, "And the best way to hide the truth . . ."

Lila finished his sentence . . . "is to discredit it."

CHAPTER 24

Alec sat with Chet and Gina on the back porch. His mom had made a special meal and invited his dad over to join them as a family before Alec left for Cincinnati. Gina still did not know anything about the adventure that Alec and Chet had been through in the past couple of weeks. But Alec felt that it was fitting for his family dinner to take place while looking out on the hill behind his house . . . his mound . . . where spirit watchers will continue to look from. As Gina began to take dishes into the house, Chet leaned over to Alec.

"Al, I am so very proud of you. I'll miss you like crazy when you leave for college, but I know that you have the integrity to follow your heart and make good decisions."

"Thanks Dad," Alec smiled. "I'm going to miss being here . . . and I hope Mom will be ok without me around."

"Don't worry, I'll stop in and check on her now and then. I want to keep an eye on the land behind the house anyway." Chet replied with a wink and twinkle in his eye.

Just then, Gina came back out, followed by Lila.

"Look who stopped by—my shopping buddy!" Gina said as she smiled at Lila. Alec was glad that his mom and Lila seemed to get along so well. They had already made plans to go to Cleveland together and go shopping after Alec left for Cincinnati. Lila needed a mother figure who would spend time with her, and Gina would need a substitute kid after Alec left.

"Chet, why don't you help me clean up and get dessert ready and we'll let the kids talk." Gina said as she picked up more dishes from the table. Chet obliged and picked up the remaining items on the table before following her in the house.

Alec and Lila had gone on the picnic that Lila had promised after Alec helped her with her truck. They found that they had a lot in common and had spent quite a bit of time together. Sam and Uncle Brooks were both happy with Alec's actions at the Native American Council building, and Alec had learned more about Chief Manitou in the past couple weeks. When Uncle Brooks took on the 'chief' persona and told stories to groups, he was educating people about the history of the ancient Ohio people. He even included some reference to spirit watchers, just to plant a seed in the minds of people who listened to him. Maybe someday people would be ready to know the truth.

Lila turned to Alec. "I'll hopefully see you again before you go, but your mom invited me to stop over for dessert after the family dinner. You know Alec, I'm really going to miss you." Lila's green eyes looked down.

"Hey now," Alec said "don't be sad, I'll be back to visit a lot and Cincinnati is only 3 and a half hours away. If your pick-up truck can survive a black cow, I'm sure it could make a trip that far."

Lila laughed, "That's true—and you know that I can find you wherever you are! Oh, that reminds me . . . I have a little going away gift for you . . ." Lila pulled a small package out of her purse and handed it to Alec. Alec opened the package to reveal a plastic miniature black colored cow, like the kind you would find in a little kid's farm play set.

Alec laughed out loud "It's the perfect reminder of our adventure!"

"I know, right?" Lila laughed along "It's nothing big, but I knew you'd think of me when you look at your black cow!"

Alec's parents came back out carrying a cake. On the top was written: 'Good Luck Alec!'

Gina was a little teary eyed as she said "Having you leave feels like the end of your childhood. But we hope that you'll have new adventures at college."

Alec smiled as he looked around at the people who would miss him. "Don't worry, nothing is really ending and I'm sure this is just the beginning of new adventures!"

EPILOGUE

As the four people laughed and talked at the bottom of the hill, a pair of wise and gentle eyes watched from the wooded area above. Peaceful in feeling that ancient areas were still safe, he turned and walked into the blackness as high branches in the trees stirred as he went.

ABOUT THE AUTHOR

Tama is an educator, mom and wife in northeastern Ohio. She teaches science, reading and history and she strives to keep young adults interested in learning about the world around them. Tama is blessed with two daughters and a wonderful husband. This is her first book.

ABOUT THE ILLUSTRATOR

Sarah Brand is a twenty year old freelance illustrator, born and raised in northern Ohio. She is currently studying at Savannah College of Art and Design(SCAD) for a Bachelors Degree in Sequential Art. Hoping to one day get into the industry and work on movies or comic books.

REFERENCES

GIANTS OF OHIO

Sutherland, Mary. Giants of Ohio and the Mound Builders. Retreived 6/12/2009 and 1/15/2011 from http://www.burlingtonnews.net/ohiogiants.html

GENERAL INFORMATION ABOUT OHIO INDIANS

Ohio Historical Society. *Historic American Indian Tribes of Ohio.* Retreived in 2009 from www.ohiohistory.org

Some places and elements in this story are accurate, however this story is a work of fiction.

Tama

Geography connection:

Look on an Ohio map. List cities named in the book that are real places.

List one Highway that really exists and is also used in this story.

What region of the United States is Ohio located in?

What is the climate in Ohio like?

History connection:

Use resources to find the names of at least 2 different tribes of Native people who once lived in North Eastern Ohio.

What other regions in the United States have evidence of mound building societies?

About what period of time were the Ohio mound builders active?

What type of dwelling did mound builders live in?

From what archaeologists and historians have determined, what foods did tribes of Ohio mound builders eat?

Were they nomadic or sedentary people?

Language Arts connection:

Write the next chapter—What happens next?

Find 5 words that you are not familiar with. Define each and list two synonyms and two antonyms for each.